Dear Parents and Educators,

Welcome to Penguin Young Readers! As parents and educators, you know that each child develops at his or her own pace—in terms of speech, critical thinking, and, of course, reading. Penguin Young Readers recognizes this fact. As a result, each Penguin Young Readers book is assigned a traditional easy-to-read level (1–4) as well as a Guided Reading Level (A–P). Both of these systems will help you choose the right book for your child. Please refer to the back of each book for specific leveling information. Penguin Young Readers features esteemed authors and illustrators, stories about favorite characters, fascinating nonfiction, and more!

## Skylanders Universe™
## Skylanders Academy

This book is perfect for a **Transitional Reader** who:
- can read multisyllable and compound words;
- can read words with prefixes and suffixes;
- is able to identify story elements (beginning, middle, end, plot, setting, characters, problem, solution); and
- can understand different points of view.

Here are some **activities** you can do during and after reading this book:
- -ed Endings: List all the words in the story that have an -ed ending. On a separate piece of paper, write the root word next to the word with the -ed ending. The chart below will get you started:

| word with an -ed ending | root word |
| --- | --- |
| dreamed | dream |
| helped | help |
| burrowed | burrow |

- Problem/Solution: In this story, the entrance to Kaos's cave is too small for the Minis to fit through. This is the problem. Discuss their solution.

Remember, sharing the love of reading with a child is the best gift you can give!

—Bonnie Bader, EdM
  Penguin Young Readers program

*Penguin Young Readers are leveled by independent reviewers applying the sta
and Gay Su Pinnell in *Matching Books to Readers: Using Leveled Books in Guided Reading*, ...

D0205192

PENGUIN YOUNG READERS
An Imprint of Penguin Random House LLC

© 2015 Activision Publishing, Inc. SKYLANDERS UNIVERSE is a trademark and ACTIVISION is a registered trademark of Activision Publishing, Inc. Published by Penguin Young Readers, an imprint of Penguin Random House LLC, 345 Hudson Street, New York, New York 10014. Printed in the USA.

ISBN 978-0-448-48770-0                                                    10 9 8 7 6 5 4 3 2 1

PENGUIN YOUNG READERS

LEVEL
3

TRANSITIONAL READER

# SKYLANDERS UNIVERSE

# SKYLANDERS ACADEMY

illustrated by Caravan Studio

Penguin Young Readers
An Imprint of Penguin Random House

# Glossary

**Elements** are what give the Skylanders their powers. There are 10 Elements: Magic, Earth, Water, Fire, Tech, Undead, Life, Air, Light, and Dark.

**Kaos** is an evil Portal Master. His goal is to defeat the Skylanders and take over Skylands.

**Master Eon** is known as the greatest Portal Master ever. He exists only in spirit form, but is still able to guide the Skylanders.

**Minis** are smaller versions of Skylanders who are training to become full-fledged Skylanders.

**Molekin** are peaceful creatures who dig caves in Skylands.

**Portal Masters** are very special magical beings who have the power to summon Skylanders and teleport them through time and space.

**Skylanders** are heroes who use their Elemental powers to protect Skylands.

**Skylanders Academy** is the school where Skylanders train and learn new skills.

**Skylands** is a magical world made up of many floating islands. It's where the Skylanders live.

The Skylander Minis had dreamed about becoming heroes all their lives. Many of the experienced Skylanders, like Terrafin, helped train the Minis at Skylanders Academy.

Terrabite and Weeruptor were practicing their Earth and Fire attacks together. Terrabite, a small dirt shark, burrowed into the ground, then jumped high into the air, landing with a big belly flop.

Weeruptor turned himself into a pool of hot lava and back again.

"All right!" said Terrafin as he observed his students. "Master Eon will make you Skylanders in no time."

Weeruptor and Terrabite bumped
their fists together. Terrabite was
glad that Terrafin, his greatest hero,
was proud of him.

Suddenly, a deep voice came from the sky. It was Master Eon, the Portal Master who called upon the Skylanders whenever there was trouble.

"Terrafin!" he said. "I need you
to gather all your students and
come with me. Kaos has invaded a
Molekin village, and only the Minis
can stop him."

What could the Minis do that experienced Skylanders couldn't? Still, Terrafin knew he had to trust Eon.

"Attention, all students," he shouted. "Come to the Portal right now—we have been called on a mission!"

"A mission?" said Eye Small,
looking around with his one eyeball
in excitement.

"Excellent!" said Mini Jini, a
Magic ninja genie.

Terrafin and the Minis took the
Portal to a dry, rocky island with a
large mountain at the center.

A nervous Molekin ran up to them.
"Thank goodness you've come!"
he said. "Kaos and his minions used
Dark Magic to hide in the mountain.
We don't know what they want, but it
can't be good!"

"The tunnels deep inside the mountain are too small—even for us!" said the Molekin. "They used to be bigger, but parts of them have caved in."

"We can help you!" said Pet Vac bravely. "We may be tiny, but we have plenty of courage!"

"Stick together and be safe!" said Terrafin as the Minis climbed into the tunnel.

Soon, the space became very small, and they could hear Kaos and his Trolls laughing nearby.

"Once I put on my new mind-control hat, I will force the Molekin to become my servants, and then nobody will be able to stop me from ruling Skylands. HA-HA!" said Kaos.

When the Minis reached Kaos's cave, they saw that the entrance was too small for any of them to fit through. But Terrabite had an idea.

"I can dig it!" he yelled, diving through the dirt and belly flopping onto Kaos, just like he had practiced.

"EEEEEEE!" shrieked Kaos, dropping his magical hat in shock. "A Skylander! How did you get into my super-secret lair?" The Trolls jumped back in surprise.

"But wait," Kaos said. "You are too small to be a Skylander. Get out of here before I kick you out, puny dirt shark!"

"You'll need to deal with us first, then!" shouted Weeruptor.

"Any last wishes?" Mini Jini said, pulling a magical purple orb out of thin air.

"Go away and leave me to my evil plans, you tiny things!" Kaos said.

"Wish not granted!" Mini Jini shouted, throwing the orb at Kaos.

Pet Vac used his vacuum jet to push
the Trolls away from his friends.

Kaos screamed as Eye Small's tiny eyeball came flying right at him.

"Eye see you, Kaos!" said Eye Small.

Weeruptor started to erupt, and his hot lava puddle soon reached Kaos's feet, where it melted the mind-control hat.

"No! My hat! Minions—to the Dark Portal!" Kaos yelled to the Trolls.

Kaos and the Trolls scrambled to
the Portal as the Minis each used
their special powers.

When the villains had disappeared,
the Minis came back out through
the tunnel. Terrafin and Master Eon
were there, smiling.

"Now *that's* what real heroes look like!" said Terrafin.

"Hear, hear!" said Master Eon. "Which is why I'm making you all official Skylanders. Congratulations!"

The Minis cheered. They knew their adventures were only just beginning.